Nell & the Circus of Dreams

OXFORD
UNIVERSITY PRESS

Great Clarendon Street, Oxford OX2 6DP

Oxford University Press is a department of the University of Oxford.
It furthers the University's objective of excellence in research, scholarship,
and education by publishing worldwide. Oxford is a registered trade mark of
Oxford University Press in the UK and in certain other countries

British Library Cataloguing in Publication Data available

ISBN: 978-0-19-276594-9

3 5 7 9 10 8 6 4 2

Printed in China

Paper used in the production of this book is a natural, recyclable product made
from wood grown in sustainable forests. The manufacturing process conforms
to the environmental regulations of the country of origin

For Daniella Ghionea—N.G.

For Great Grandpa and Great Grandma xx—B.M.S.

Nell Gifford & Briony May Smith

Nell & the Circus of Dreams

OXFORD

UNIVERSITY PRESS

That summer Nell's mother was so ill that she did not get out of bed.

The farmhouse was quiet and Nell was sad . . .

. . . but then she found something in the dusty farmyard that would come to make her happy.

A tiny, lost chick.

Nell took the chick inside, and they became friends.
Nell called her Rosebud.

Rosebud knew all of Nell's dreams and all of her fears. She carried them in her soft, warm feathers and she kept Nell's dreams safe. Nell did not like to think of losing Rosebud.

But the moment that Rosebud disappeared was the moment that the magic started happening . . .

At sunset Rosebud had settled at the end of Nell's bed, as she always did.

By sunrise . . .

she was gone.

Nell ran across the flagstone
floor to the garden,

and then out
into the farmyard,

and the meadows beyond.

The dew soaked her feet and her dreams
were scattered all about.

As Nell searched, she found herself among huge, red, wooden wheels. Smells of coffee and toast mixed with hedgerow smells of cow parsley and crushed grass. *Is someone making breakfast?* wondered Nell.

The air was ringing with the sound of hammers hitting metal stakes. What could it be?

It was a circus!

The tent went up like a balloon, and when Nell peeped inside she could see laughing girls hanging scarlet velvets and gold cables and twinkling lights on silver ropes.

Nell watched and helped
the bright, dusty people.

She sat on a set of little steps
that led to a house on wheels.
For a moment it felt like home.
But then Nell thought of her
mum and Rosebud and she cried.

A giant man with golden arms
picked Nell up. His voice was kind.

In a moment Nell was inside the little house with a whole circus family.
The man with the golden arms, a woman with jewels in her hair, and seven children.

The children all spoke at once in musical tones,
and used words that Nell could not recognise.

'I have lost my chicken,' said Nell.

The children could not understand her. They found a stub
of pencil and a piece of card, and Nell drew a chicken.
But the children shook their heads.

Then the music started,
and it sounded to Nell like
a thousand instruments.

Nell followed the family
as they dashed out the door . . .

. . . and into the tent. In the velvet darkness behind the curtain, Nell was filled with the drumming music of the show.

Horses and acrobats streamed past into the gold and the music and the light.

Nell's heart was beating fast. The children juggled silver hoops
and danced on the back of a white horse.

The mother sailed through the air and someone took Nell's hand as if to say,
'Come on, fly with us!' For a dizzying moment Nell felt as if she was flying.

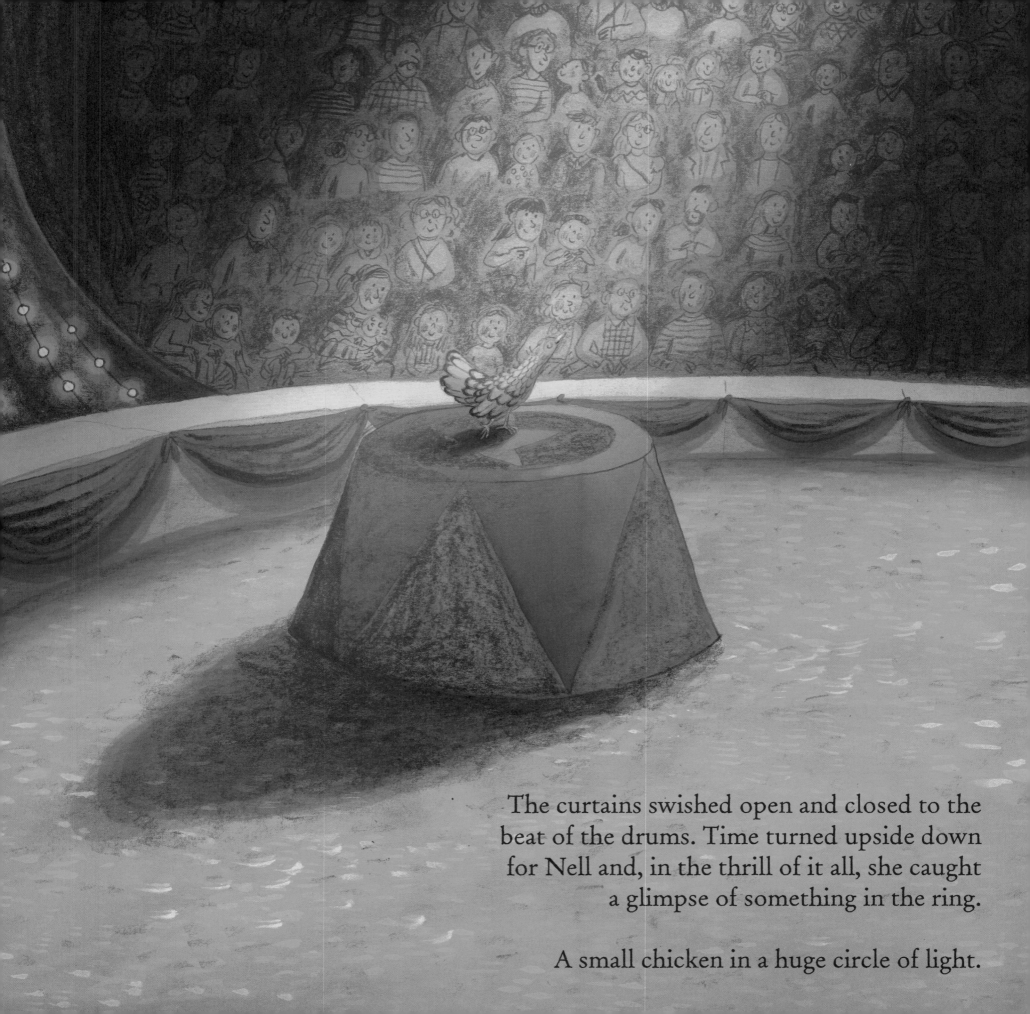

The curtains swished open and closed to the
beat of the drums. Time turned upside down
for Nell and, in the thrill of it all, she caught
a glimpse of something in the ring.

A small chicken in a huge circle of light.

'Rosebud!' Nell cried.

Then the children lifted Nell,
and the golden man lifted the children,
and they all balanced in the middle
of the tent held up by the laughing
and clapping and cheering.

Nell wished that this
beautiful circus of dreams
could last forever.

After the show, the tent was dropped into silken bags,
a hundred arms lifted the bags into wooden carts,
and in a clop of horses' hooves and a creak of leather . . .

. . . the circus was gone.

A golden circle of sawdust
in the bright green grass
was all that was left.

Nell slowly brushed glitter from
her cheeks. 'Come on, Rosebud,'
said Nell. 'Let's go home.'

They left a trail of ribbons and sequins
as they traced their path back through the dew.

When she reached the garden,
Nell ran into her mother's arms.

'Where have you two chickens been?'
asked Nell's mother, as she gently pulled
a strand of ribbon from Nell's hair.

'To the circus,' Nell said. How she wished
that she could visit the circus again,
with her mother and Rosebud.

But the circus never returned to the farm,
and the memory faded like a beautiful dream.

It didn't matter, though,
because the rest of that summer, and summers beyond . . .

Nell and Rosebud made their own.